THE **Emotion** OCEAN

Jellyfish Feels Jealous

by Katie Woolley and David Arumi

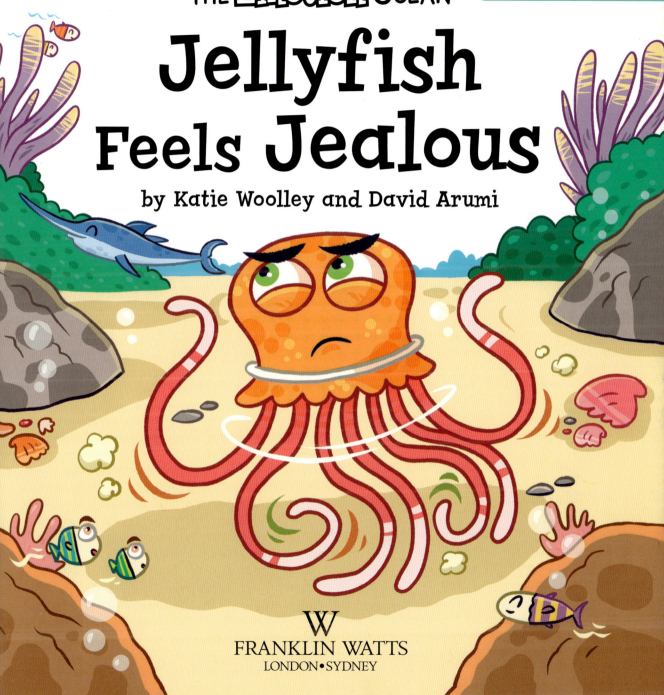

W

FRANKLIN WATTS

LONDON • SYDNEY

Class One was very excited. It was the school swim team trials and everyone wanted to make the team.

Jellyfish
Feels Jealous

Franklin Watts
First published in Great Britain in 2021 by The Watts Publishing Group

Credits
Series Editor: Sarah Peutrill
Series Designer: Sarah Peden

ISBN: 978 1 4451 7455 6 (hardback)
ISBN: 978 1 4451 7456 3 (paperback)

Printed in China

Franklin Watts
An imprint of
Hachette Children's Group
Part of The Watts Publishing Group
Carmelite House
50 Victoria Embankment
London EC4Y 0DZ

An Hachette UK Company
www.hachette.co.uk

w.hachettechildrens.co.uk

Swordfish had on a **brand-new** pair of goggles.

Starfish had a *lucky* swimming cap.

Jellyfish didn't have new googles or a lucky hat.
It's not fair, he thought.

"It's time to line up, everyone!" called Mr Narwhal.

The animals swam off.

As they got to the finish line, Swordfish and Shark were **neck and neck**.

But Jellyfish could not keep up with his friends.

Suddenly, Swordfish burst ahead. Her nose crossed the finish line first.

All the class clapped and cheered.

"You were amazing, Swordfish!"
said Whale.

Jellyfish watched his friends congratulate Swordfish.

He'd wanted to **win** and have everyone clap him on the back.

Before Jellyfish could stop himself, he shouted, "Swordfish won because her silly nose is so *BIG!*"

Swordfish's grin fell. She swam slowly and sadly into the classroom.

Well, it's true, thought Jellyfish.

Jellyfish spent the morning in a bad mood.

He couldn't get his spellings right.

He even mixed up his tentacles and got his sums wrong.

"Are you all right, Jellyfish?" asked Mr Narwhal. "You don't seem yourself."

Jellyfish wasn't all right. In fact, he felt dreadful.

"I wanted to win the race and get on the swim team," he said. "But Swordfish won."

"Swordfish is very good at swimming," Mr Narwhal agreed. "She **should** be on the team."

"I know," said Jellyfish. "But I felt so jealous that I was unkind to her."

"We all feel jealous sometimes," said Mr Narwhal. "But we are all good at different things. No one else can jump as high as you!"

Jellyfish thought for a moment. "Maybe I should try out for the gymnastics team!" said Jellyfish.

"That's a good idea," nodded Mr Narwhal. "But you need to put things right with Swordfish, too."

Jellyfish bobbed off to tell Swordfish he was sorry.

That afternoon, Swordfish was training with the swim team.

When Swordfish won her race, Jellyfish jumped up and down, shouting, "Go, Swordfish, go!"

Swordfish beamed as her biggest supporter jumped higher than anyone else!

Emotions are BIG!

Your feelings are a big part of you, just like they are a big part of Jellyfish and his friends. Look at the pictures and talk about these feelings. Here are some questions to help you:

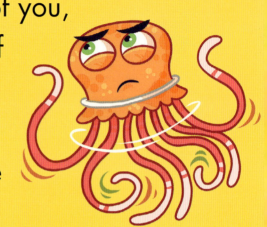

What emotion did Jellyfish feel when he saw everyone in their new swimming hats and googles?

How did Swordfish feel when Jellyfish was unkind to her?

What did Mr Narwhal
help Jellyfish to realise?

How did Jellyfish
put things right with
Swordfish?

How did Jellyfish and
Swordfish feel at the
end of the story?

What could YOU
do next time you
feel jealous?

Let's Talk About Feelings

The Emotion Ocean series has been written to help young children begin to understand their own feelings, and how those feelings and subsequent actions affect themselves and others.

It provides a starting point for parents, carers and teachers to discuss BIG feelings with little learners. The series is set in the ocean with a class of animal friends who experience these big emotions in familiar, everyday scenarios.

Jellyfish Feels Jealous

This story looks at feeling jealous, how it makes you feel, how you react to the feeling of being jealous and how you can help overcome the emotion and begin to feel happy for yourself and for other people.

The book aims to encourage children to identify their own feelings, consider how feelings can affect their own happiness and the happiness of others, and offer simple tools to help manage their emotions.

How to use the book

The book is designed for adults to share with either an individual child, or a group of children, and as a starting point for discussion.

Choose a time when you and the children are relaxed and have time to share the story.

Before reading the story:

• Spend time looking at the illustrations and talking about what the book might be about before reading it together.

• Encourage children to employ a 'phonics-first' approach to tackling new words by sounding them out.

After reading the story:

• Talk about the story with the children. Ask them to describe Jellyfish's feelings. Ask them if they have ever felt jealous. Can they remember when and why?

• Ask the children why they think it is important to understand their feelings. Does it make them feel better to understand why they feel the way they do in certain situations? Does it help them get along with others?

• Place the children into groups. Ask them to think of a scenario when somebody might feel jealous. What could they do to make themselves feel better? (For example, make a list of things they are thankful for.)

• At the end of the session, invite a spokesperson from each group to read out their ideas to the others. Then discuss the different ideas as a whole class.